# Awesome ENGINEERING

# BRIDGES

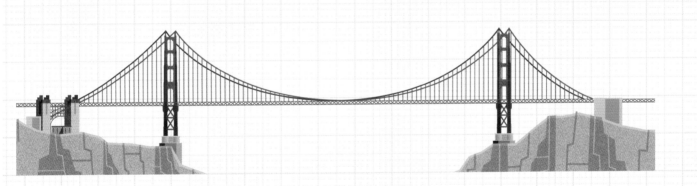

**SALLY SPRAY**
**WITH ARTWORK BY MARK RUFFLE**

W
FRANKLIN WATTS
LONDON · SYDNEY

Franklin Watts

First published in Great Britain in 2017
by The Watts Publishing Group
Copyright © The Watts Publishing Group, 2017

All rights reserved.

Series editor: Paul Rockett
Series design and illustration: Mark Ruffle
www.rufflebrothers.com
Consultant:
Andrew Woodward BEng (Hons) CEng MICE FCIArb

HB ISBN 978 1 4451 5529 6
PB ISBN 978 1 4451 5530 2

Printed in China

Franklin Watts
An imprint of
Hachette Children's Group
Part of The Watts Publishing Group
Carmelite House
50 Victoria Embankment
London EC4Y 0DZ
An Hachette UK Company
www.hachette.co.uk
www.franklinwatts.co.uk

Every attempt has been made to
clear copyright. Should there be any
inadvertent omission please apply to
the publisher for rectification.

Picture credits:
Leonid Andronov/Shutterstock: 6;
Vichaya Kiatying-Angsulee/Alamy: 29cl;
Anyaivanova/Shutterstock: 14; unknown
photographer for Benjamin Baker/
Wikimedia Commons: 11; Andrey Bayda/
Shutterstock: 9; Ben Bryant/Shutterstock:
28tr; Cpaulfell/Dreamstime: 19;
Dvoevnore/Shutterstock: 13; Mary Evans
PL: 10; Olga Gavrilova/ShutterstockL: 29cr;
Joyfull/Shutterstock: 26; Michal Kniti/
Dreamstime: 28tc; Nicola Messana Photos/
Shutterstock: 7; R.M.Nunes/Shutterstock:
23; PHB.cz (Richard Semik)/Shutterstock:
24; Terry Reimink/Dreamstime: 29c;
seanelliottphotography/Shutterstock: 28tl;
Hiroshi Tanaka/Dreamstime: 21; Andrew
Zarivny/Shutterstock: 16.

# CONTENTS

# GET OVER IT!

Bridges create connections between places, allowing people to travel and trade. We have been building bridges for thousands of years. As building techniques have developed, so have the shapes, the weight bridges can carry and the lengths they can span.

## EARLY BRIDGES

One of the earliest surviving bridges is the Arkadiko Bridge in Greece, built around the 13th century BCE. This small arch bridge is 4 m high and 22 m long. It was built from limestone rocks packed tightly together and held in place by their weight. Built over a small stream, it let chariots speed along on their journey and even had curbs in place to guide the wheels.

The **Iron Bridge** was the first arch bridge to be made from cast iron. It was opened in 1781 and crosses the River Severn in England. Iron is not a strong enough material to be used for long bridges; this bridge is 30 m long.

The world's first completely welded bridge is the 1929, 27-m long **Maurzyce Bridge** in Poland. Steel welding has allowed engineers to build bridges in all shapes and sizes with far greater spans.

The **Alcántara Bridge** in Spain was built by the Romans between CE 104 and 106, using stone and a type of cement, called pozzolana, made from volcanic ash.

The development of steel meant bridges could be made longer and stronger. Gustave Eiffel, designer of the Eiffel Tower, built the magnificent **Garabit Viaduct** (1895). This arched truss bridge spans a large valley and carries trains travelling to and from the south of France.

The **Anji Bridge**, in China, was finished in CE 605 and is still standing over 14 centuries later. Designed by Li Chun, the curve is made from limestone fixed with iron. When the water rises, it flows through the top arches.

0   25   50   75   100   125   150   175   200   225   250   275

Length in metres

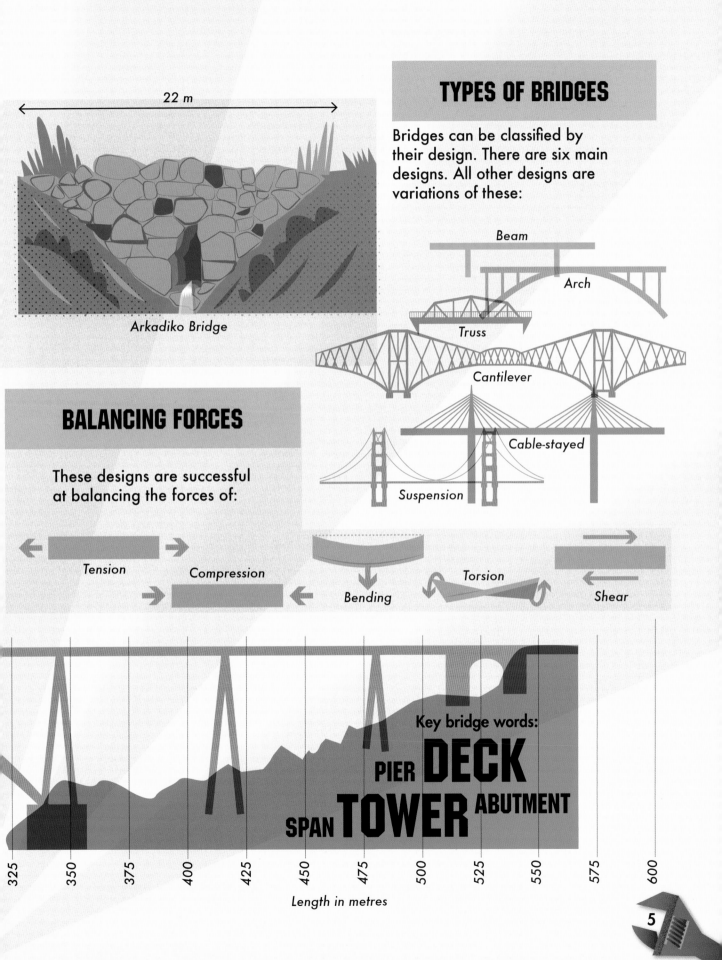

22 m

Arkadiko Bridge

## TYPES OF BRIDGES

Bridges can be classified by their design. There are six main designs. All other designs are variations of these:

Beam

Arch

Truss

Cantilever

Cable-stayed

Suspension

## BALANCING FORCES

These designs are successful at balancing the forces of:

Tension

Compression

Bending

Torsion

Shear

Key bridge words:

PIER **DECK**

SPAN **TOWER** ABUTMENT

325   350   375   400   425   450   475   500   525   550   575   600

*Length in metres*

# SI-O-SEH POL

Si-o-Seh Pol is a magnificent example of an arch bridge. Built between 1599 and 1602 from stone and brick, it stretches across the Zayandeh river in Isfahan, Iran. Its name means 'bridge of 33 arches' in the Farsi language, as this is the number of big arches in the design.

*There are two tiers of arches along the bridge.*

## BUILDING BRIEF

Construct a bridge to cross a river and unite the north and south sides of Isfahan. It should be sturdy enough to withstand the fast river, with high sides to protect pedestrians from strong wind and sun.

**Builder:** Ostad Hossein Banna (overseen by Allah Verdi Khan Undiladze)

**Location:** Isfahan, Iran

## WHAT'S SO GOOD ABOUT AN ARCH BRIDGE?

Arch bridges neatly distribute the compression force both through the arch – into the supporting piers – and along the length. The piers are held in place at the ends of the bridge by abutments. These stop the arch from spreading out and collapsing.

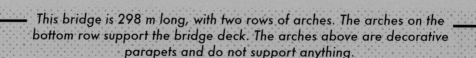

*This bridge is 298 m long, with two rows of arches. The arches on the bottom row support the bridge deck. The arches above are decorative parapets and do not support anything.*

## FOUNDATIONS

Bridges must be built on strong foundations sunk into the ground. To build the Si-o-Seh Pol, the river was diverted so the foundations could be dug down to the bedrock. Its foundations are lined with earthenware pipes filled with rubble and mud. This supports the stone piers that in turn support the arches. The abutments were put in place to support each end of the bridge ready for the next stage of the build.

*The deck of the bridge carries the 'live load' of pedestrians.*

## KEYSTONE

The last stone to be put in place is called the keystone. During construction, the bridge's arch has to be supported from underneath. The keystone is the last piece of the jigsaw. Once it is put in place the supports can be taken away and the arch becomes self-supporting.

For every force (action), there is an equal and opposite reaction. So, as the load pushes the keystone downwards, the force is distributed down through the arch, and the ground pushes back through the bridge's arch to the keystone. The force also pushes sideways into the abutments, which apply a balancing force, helping to keep the bridge stable.

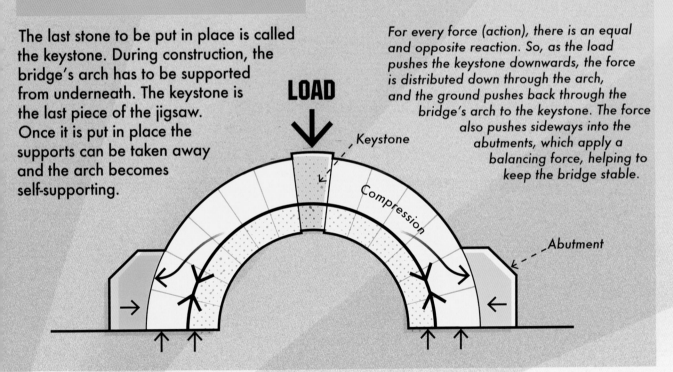

LOAD

Keystone

Compression

Abutment

# BROOKLYN BRIDGE

When it was opened in 1883, the Brooklyn Bridge in New York City, USA, was the longest suspension bridge in the world. It was a huge project. But it was a dangerous project too – more than 20 construction workers died.

## BUILDING BRIEF

Design and build a bridge to cross the East River, linking Manhattan with Brooklyn. It will replace the overused and unreliable ferry service and help businesses to survive in Brooklyn.

**Engineers:** John A Roebling, Washington Roebling, Emily Roebling

**Location:** New York City, USA

Length 1,825 m

## CAISSONS

The foundations for the enormous bridge were dug out of the riverbed using a device called a caisson. Caissons resemble an upturned wooden barrel open at the bottom. To sink them to the bottom, the stone towers were built on top, pushing them into the silt of the riverbed. Air was pumped in, giving the workers, nicknamed 'sandhogs', access to dig out the silt. Building of the towers continued on top as the workers dug down to the bedrock. Once the work was complete the air space was filled with stones to complete the construction of the towers.

# CABLES

The suspension bridge's huge granite towers stretch 84 m above the water and support the main steel cables. These are anchored at each end of the bridge to stone weighing 54,400 tonnes. The main cables are made from 5,434 separate steel wires that were spun together on site. More steel cables attach the bridge deck to the main cables, in a vertical and diagonal pattern.

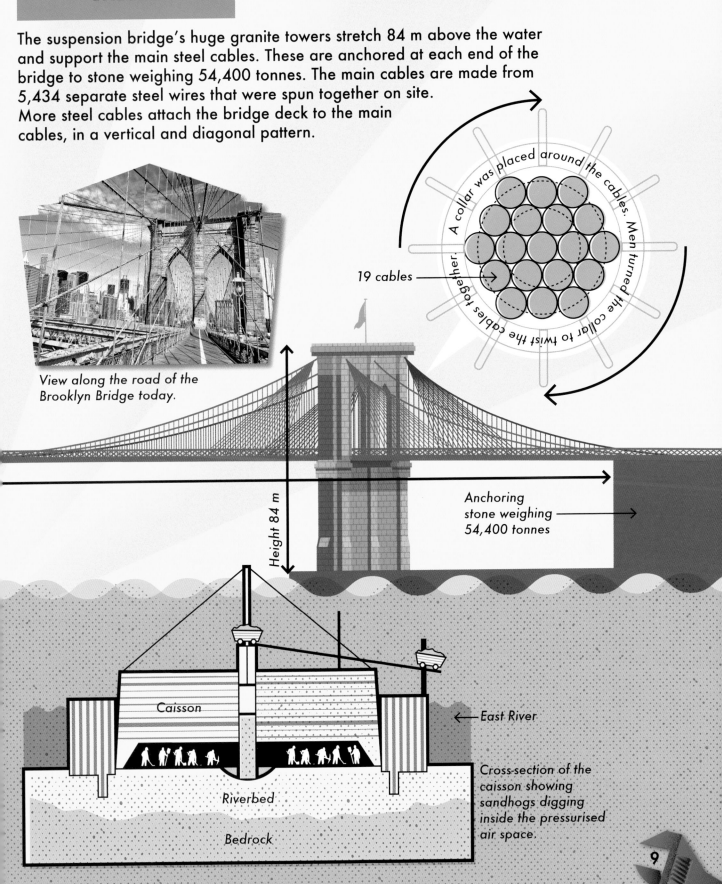

View along the road of the Brooklyn Bridge today.

A collar was placed around the cables. Men turned the collar to twist the cables together.

19 cables

Height 84 m

Anchoring stone weighing 54,400 tonnes

Caisson

East River

Riverbed

Bedrock

Cross-section of the caisson showing sandhogs digging inside the pressurised air space.

# FORTH BRIDGE

This majestic rail bridge crosses the Firth of Forth in Scotland and carries up to 200 trains per day. It opened in 1890 after nearly a hundred years of planning and eight years of building work.

*The bridge during construction.*

## BUILDING BRIEF

Design a rail bridge to cross the estuary, replacing the ferry links. Take into account the unsupportive riverbed, the high winds and the heavy loads of freight to be transported safely across.

**Engineer:** Sir John Fowler

**Designer:** Sir Benjamin Baker

**Location:** Firth of Forth, Scotland, UK

## TOWERS AND TRUSSES

Three supporting towers, resting on granite piers, supported the two truss girders – this formed the link spans connecting the south and north banks. An intricate network of steel trusses was then threaded through the length carrying the two railway tracks along the middle. This clever design meant the end towers could be built on the solid ground of the banks, with the middle tower resting on a natural island in the middle of the river. This avoided foundations in the unstable riverbed.

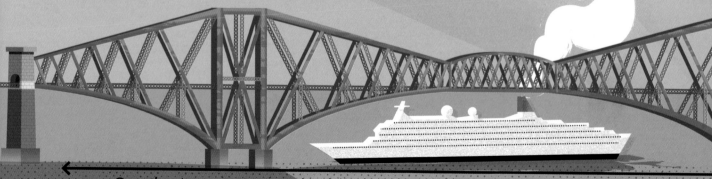

*Once the piers were constructed and the steel towers added, the cantilever supports were built outwards to form three massive diamond-shaped structures.*

# THE CANTILEVERED SOLUTION

In the 19th century, engineers had discovered that a longer span for a bridge could be achieved with a cantilevered design. This is achieved by anchoring the bridge platform at one end, with further strengthening from staggered supports, making a structure like a giant diving board. If two of these spans were put together the bridge could be really long and super strong. This was ideal for heavy rail bridges. It was this cantilevered design that was chosen by Sir John Fowler for the Forth Bridge.

*The bridge engineers Sir John Fowler and Sir Benjamin Baker demonstrate how their bridge works with rope, bricks and chairs. The weight of assistant Kaichi Watanabe, in the middle, is carried as compression through the lower beams whilst the men's outstretched arms stop him from swaying.*

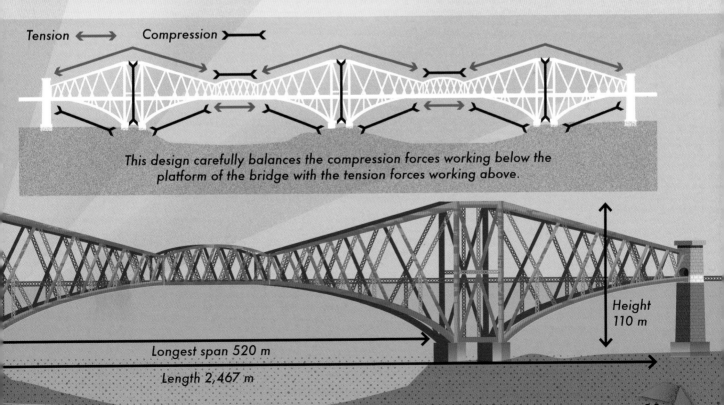

Tension ⟷    Compression ⟩—⟨

*This design carefully balances the compression forces working below the platform of the bridge with the tension forces working above.*

Height 110 m

*Longest span 520 m*

*Length 2,467 m*

# VIZCAYA BRIDGE

Built in 1893, the Vizcaya Bridge crosses the Nervión River in Spain. It was the world's first transporter bridge, carrying traffic across the river on a suspended gondola. It's still in use today.

## BUILDING BRIEF

Build a bridge to connect the towns of Portugalete and Gexto, in the Biscay province of Spain. Make sure tall ships can sail underneath.

**Designer:** Alberto de Palacio

**Engineer:** Ferdinand Arnodin

**Location:** Biscay, Spain

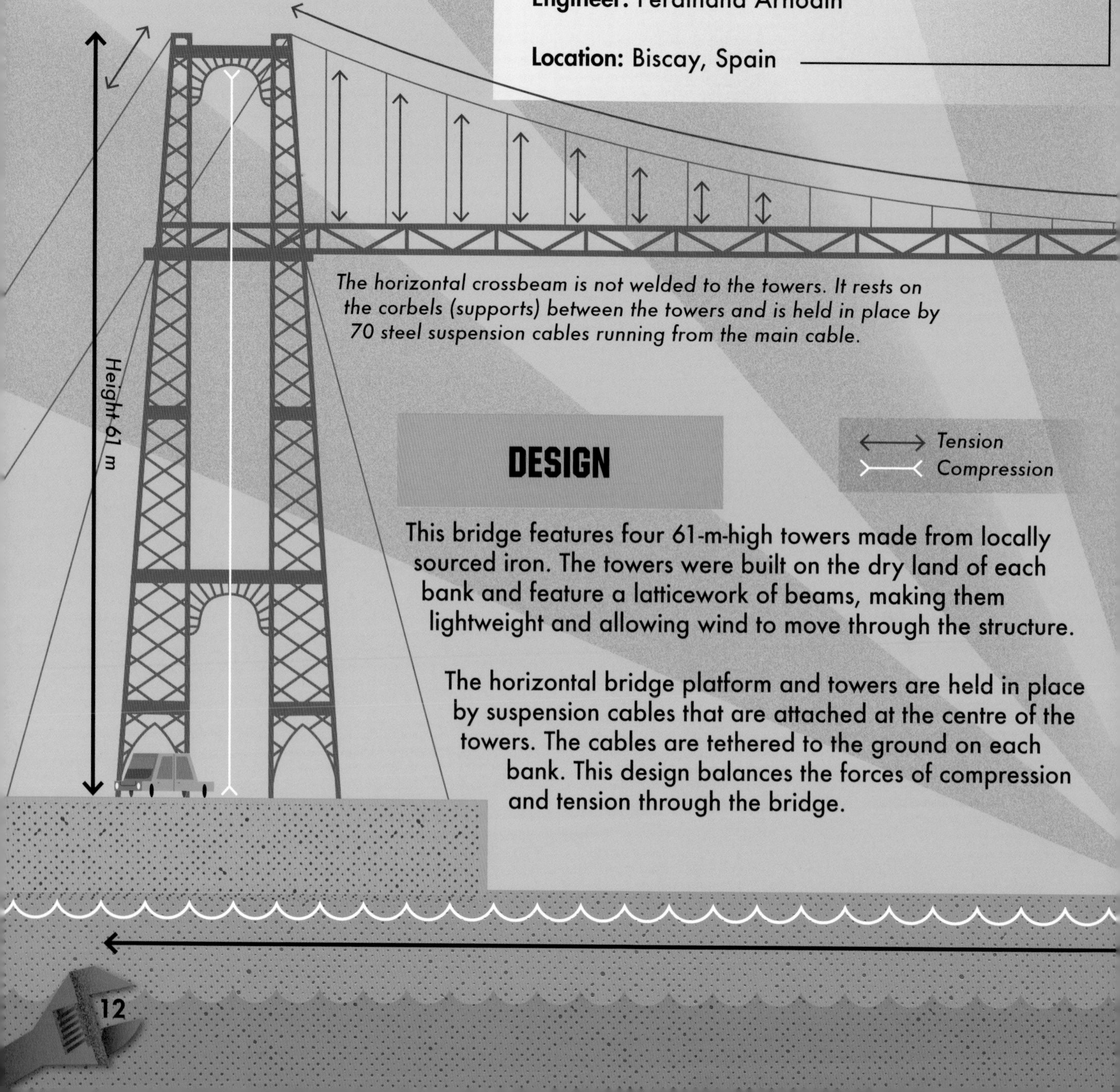


*The horizontal crossbeam is not welded to the towers. It rests on the corbels (supports) between the towers and is held in place by 70 steel suspension cables running from the main cable.*

## DESIGN

This bridge features four 61-m-high towers made from locally sourced iron. The towers were built on the dry land of each bank and feature a latticework of beams, making them lightweight and allowing wind to move through the structure.

The horizontal bridge platform and towers are held in place by suspension cables that are attached at the centre of the towers. The cables are tethered to the ground on each bank. This design balances the forces of compression and tension through the bridge.

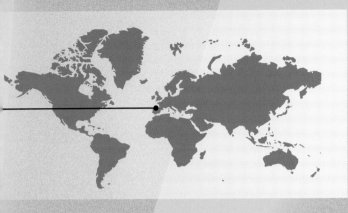

The gondola dangles below the Vizcaya Bridge.

# HANGING BRIDGE

Locally, the bridge is called Puente Colgante, which is Spanish for 'hanging bridge'.

The gondola hangs on twisted steel cables.

Unlike a traditional suspension bridge, the traffic does not move across the top, but underneath it on a cable car, called a gondola. The gondola can carry 200 people, six cars and six bicycles on each 90-second crossing. Originally a steam engine pulled the gondola; this was changed to an electric system in 1901.

Length 160 m

# TOWER BRIDGE

Tower Bridge is a major landmark in London, UK. Opened in 1894, it's a combination of two bridge styles. It's a suspension bridge, featuring the famous towers, with a bascule bridge linking them. This swings upwards to allow boats to continue up the river.

Tower Bridge, with the road bridge lowered for traffic to cross the river

## BUILDING BRIEF

Build a road and pedestrian bridge to cross the River Thames. It must allow access for sailing ships to pass under and along the busy river.

**Designer:** Sir Horace Jones

**Engineer:** Sir John Wolfe Barry

**Location:** London, England, UK

## WINNING DESIGN

Architects competed to design a bridge to cross the River Thames – there were over 50 ideas! The winning design has two bridge towers, connected by a horizontal walkway, with the bridge-lifting mechanism hidden away in the base of the towers. These are supported by two sets of double cables stretching to smaller towers at each end of the bridge. The double cables are joined together by a criss-cross of bracings connecting to the bridge deck below.

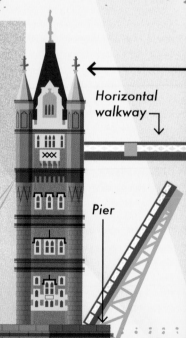

Horizontal walkway

Pier

*Bracing*

## CONSTRUCTION

The towers are supported on two massive piers (the foundations) made from over 700,000 tonnes of concrete. These were sunk into the riverbed at the beginning of the construction using caissons – it took four years just to do this! The towers and framework of the bridge were constructed from 11,000 tonnes of steel. Each tower has four upright steel pillars bolted to the granite piers.

## BASCULE MECHANISM

*Bascule* comes from the French word for 'seesaw'. The deck of the bridge is made of two enormous pivoting seesaws. While 30 m of each bridge deck is visible, the other 18 m is hidden within the bascule pit and provides the counterweight to the rising part. It is further weighted on the short end with lead and iron.

The rising parts of the bridge were originally powered by a hydraulic system that pumped water into an enclosed system raising the bridge. It was powered by steam engines on the south shore. The bridge could be opened in less than a minute. Today the steam and water system has been replaced by a mechanism powered by electricity and oil.

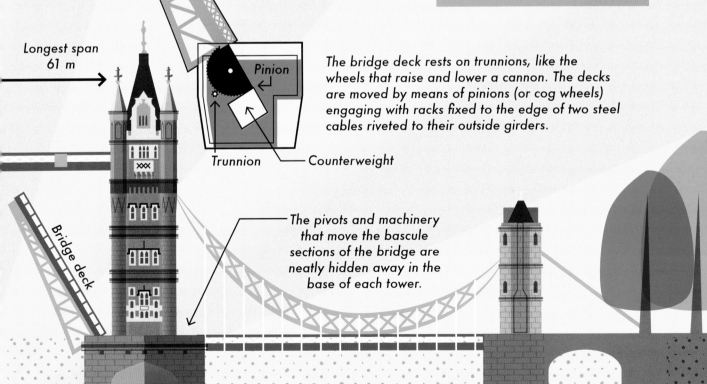

Bridge deck

Longest span
61 m

Pinion

The bridge deck rests on trunnions, like the wheels that raise and lower a cannon. The decks are moved by means of pinions (or cog wheels) engaging with racks fixed to the edge of two steel cables riveted to their outside girders.

Trunnion — Counterweight

The pivots and machinery that move the bascule sections of the bridge are neatly hidden away in the base of each tower.

Bridge deck

244 m

# GOLDEN GATE BRIDGE

When it was completed in 1937, the Golden Gate Bridge in San Francisco, USA, was the longest bridge in the world at 2,737 m, and a new landmark in engineering. The graceful design and iconic orange paintwork have made it one of the most famous and most photographed bridges in the world.

## BUILDING BRIEF

To build a bridge that spans 1.6 km of water. Must allow for changing temperatures, strong winds, sea currents and for boats to pass underneath.

The engineers decided to build a suspension bridge, as this type of bridge allows for the greatest distance to be covered with the least amount of materials and cost.

## COMPRESSION AND TENSION

A suspension bridge relies on the balanced forces of compression and tension. The weight of the deck pulls on the vertical cables. This creates tension that transfers from the vertical cables into the main cables. The main cables are secured at anchorages at each end of the bridge. The tension is concentrated here. The towers hold the main cables up in the air and transfer the full weight of the bridge into the ground.

Compression is a force that pushes down.

Tension is a force that stretches.

Span between towers 1,280 m

**Engineers:** Joseph B Strauss and Charles A Ellis

**Location:** San Francisco, California and Marin County, California, USA

## HOT AND COLD

San Francisco can get very hot and then much cooler. The engineers had to take into account the effect of changing weather on their materials.

As the temperature rises, the steel cables expand and lengthen, causing the deck to move down closer to the water. As the temperature cools, the cables contract and shrink, and the bridge deck moves up.

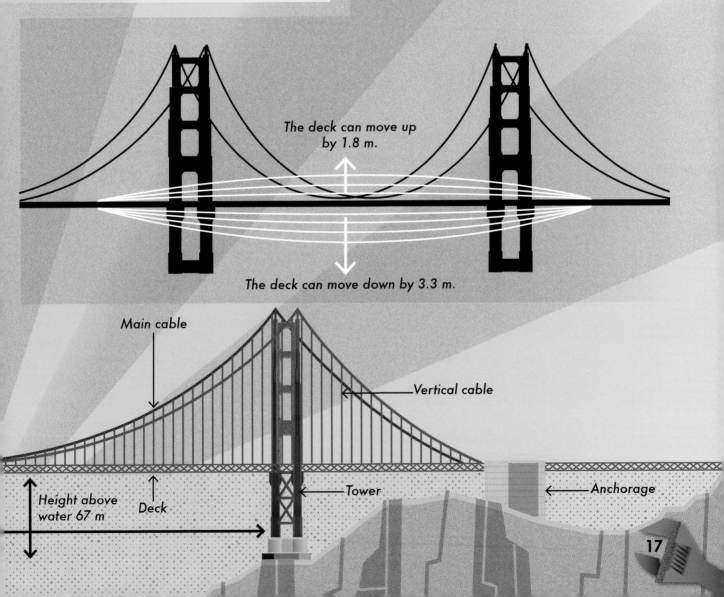

*The deck can move up by 1.8 m.*

*The deck can move down by 3.3 m.*

Main cable

Vertical cable

Height above water 67 m

Deck

Tower

Anchorage

# GOVERNOR ALBERT D ROSELLINI BRIDGE
## ALSO KNOWN AS EVERGREEN POINT FLOATING BRIDGE AND SR-520

One of the strangest solutions to bridge-building is a pontoon bridge that sits on the surface of the water. The Governor Albert D Rosellini Bridge rests on Lake Washington, USA, linking Seattle to Medina. Named the Evergreen Point Floating Bridge, it is the longest floating bridge in the world.

## BUILDING BRIEF

Design a bridge to stretch across Lake Washington. The route needs to be curved, so a suspension bridge won't work. Plus, the lake is too deep for foundations.

**Project by:** Washington State Department of Transport

**Location:** Seattle, USA

Total length
2,350 m

*The bridge deck sits on the floating pontoons.*

## OLD BRIDGE/NEW BRIDGE

The original bridge was built in 1963, but in 2016 this was replaced by a new version right beside it. The old bridge was showing signs of wear and needed to be made larger to cope with increased traffic.

The new bridge is the longest and widest floating bridge in the world. It stretches over the lake for an astonishing 2,350 m, with a midpoint width of 35 m. It has an extra lane in each direction, plus a path for pedestrians and cyclists.

# PONTOONS

Pontoons are floating concrete blocks on which the bridge sits. A total of 77 pontoons stretch across the lake. These have hollow partitioned centres that allow them to float and keep the bridge stable.

The bridge deck floats on Lake Washington.

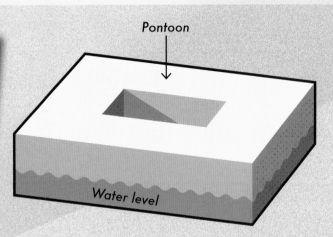

Pontoon

Water level

# ANCHORS

There are three different types of anchors used on the pontoons:

The pontoons are secured to the bottom of the lake by 58 anchors. The anchor points are located at different depths, and the chains pull at different angles, creating an enormous backbone for the bridge deck. The anchors secure the pontoons to stop the bridge floating away but also use tension forces to keep it all aligned.

**Fluke anchors** are used in softer soils, deep in the lakebed.

**Gravity anchors** are used in solid soils nearer to the shore. These are 12 m x 12 m x 7 m concrete boxes filled with rocks.

**Drilled shaft anchors** are concrete cylinders hidden in the ground near the shore.

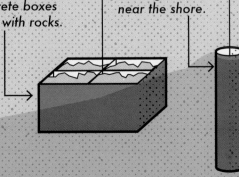

# AKASHI-KAIKYŌ BRIDGE

Although the Akashi-Kaikyō Bridge has been standing since 1998, it is still the longest, tallest and most expensive suspension bridge in the world. It stretches an incredible 3,911 m across the Akashi Strait, linking mainland Japan with Awaji Island.

## BUILDING BRIEF

Construct a safe bridge crossing from Kobe to the island of Awaji to replace ferry crossings. It has to cover a vast distance and be strong enough to withstand hurricanes, tsunamis, strong currents and earthquakes.

**Designer:** Satoshi Kashima

**Location:** Awaji Island and Kobe, Japan

## COLOSSAL FOUNDATIONS

The two gigantic towers have concrete foundations that were constructed by sinking moulds to the seabed, flooding them with seawater and then adding special concrete that could be submerged in seawater before setting. The foundations go down 60 m, the depth of a 20 storey building. Another 350,000 tonnes of concrete was used at each end of the bridge to make the cable anchor blocks.

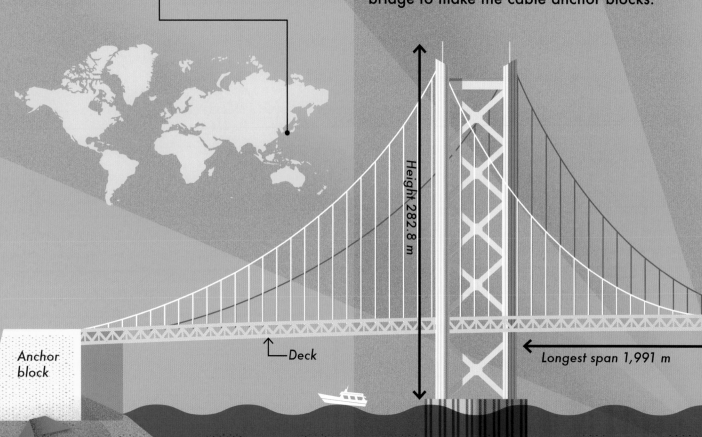

Height 282.8 m

Anchor block

Deck

Longest span 1,991 m

## TUNED MASS DAMPER TOWERS

In the towers, engineers added 20 tuned mass dampers, which are like large weighted pendulums. These sway in the opposite direction to the bridge to help control and minimise movement in strong winds.

## TRIANGULAR STRENGTH

The bridge is so long that the deck needs to be very strong to stop it twisting in the wind. The deck is a lattice of steel girders called a truss, which makes the deck very stiff. The triangular lattice adds strength, but allows the winds to whistle through. This is important, as wind speeds can be as high as 286 km/h!

When construction was underway in 1995, the main supporting towers had been finished when the Great Hanshin Earthquake struck. The towers held strong, but the earth had moved and the towers were now further apart. The span between them had to be increased by 1 m!

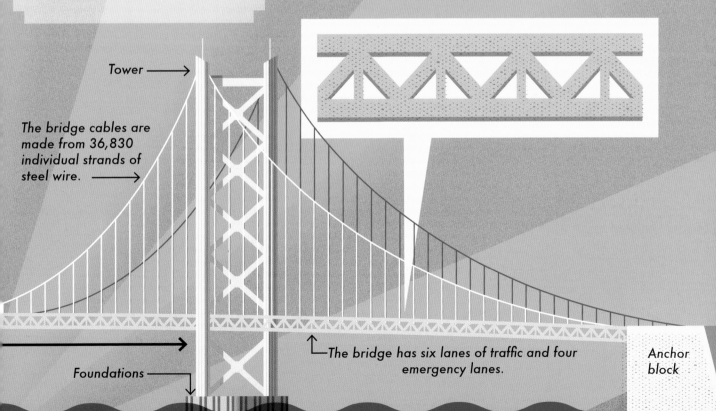

Tower ⟶

The bridge cables are made from 36,830 individual strands of steel wire. ⟶

Foundations ⟶

The bridge has six lanes of traffic and four emergency lanes.

Anchor block

# JUSCELINO KUBITSCHEK BRIDGE

The architect of the Juscelino Kubitschek Bridge wanted to make it look like a stone skimming the water. So while the components are strong and functional, it has a dynamic feel. Opened in 2002, it carries road, cycle and pedestrian traffic across Lake Paranoá in Brasília, Brazil.

## SPREADING LOAD

The design of the bridge helps to distribute the weight along the span. The load is shared between the under deck supports, the arches that criss-cross over the main bridge and the foundations. The arches support the main deck with downward cables connected to both sides of the roadway. The arches and cables are made from steel, while the supports and deck are concrete.

## BUILDING BRIEF

Win the competition to design and build a bridge to join new areas of the city across Lake Paranoá in central Brasília and be a focal point for Brazil's capital city.

**Architect:** Alexandre Chan

**Structural engineer:** Mário Vila Verde

**Location:** Brasília, Brazil

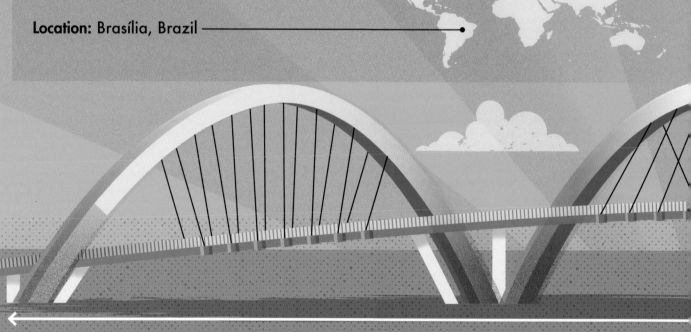

# ARCH SUPPORTS

All three arches had to be built and positioned at the same time to keep the load on the bridge balanced. The base of each arch entering the water is concrete, changing to steel as it curves overhead.

The arches were built in sections that were then floated, lifted and welded into place. Welding on the steel arch was done at night because welding would not be so successful in the high temperatures of the day.

*In 2003, the bridge won the ABCEM Award for best steel construction. It was recognised for 'showing harmony with the environment, aesthetic merit and successful community participation'.*

*The impressive Juscelino Kubitschek Bridge reflected in Lake Paranoá, Brazil.*

Height 63 m

Length 1,200 m

# MILLAU VIADUCT

Completed in 2004, the Millau Viaduct elegantly crosses the River Tarn in the south of France. It is the tallest bridge in the world, with support towers reaching 343 m in height. The structure was designed to look light and slender.

## CABLE PROTECTION

The Millau Viaduct is a cable-stayed bridge that features seven supporting towers, intersected by the road deck. From the top of the towers, 11 pairs of stays project down and fan out along the middle of the deck, holding it in place. Each stay is made from between 55 and 91 steel cables. Each cable is made from seven strands of steel wire; each strand is galvanised to protect it from corrosion, coated with petroleum wax and finally wrapped in a polythene cover.

## BUILDING BRIEF

Design and build a bridge to complete a roadway linking Paris to the Mediterranean coast and Spain, crossing the gorge of the River Tarn, between two high plateaux.

**Architect:** Norman Foster

**Engineer:** Michel Virlogeux

**Location:** Millau, France

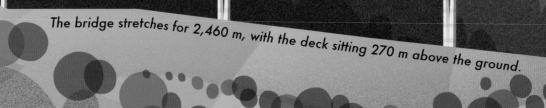

The bridge stretches for 2,460 m, with the deck sitting 270 m above the ground.

# PIERS AND PYLONS

The towering piers from the ground to the deck were made of concrete, shaped in moulds called formwork. They had to be made in stages. When one section of the concrete was set, the mould was moved up and the next lot of concrete was poured in, and slowly the piers grew taller.

The support pylons that hold the cables are made from steel and are an integral part of the bridge deck. These pylon and deck pieces were built on land and then pushed into place along temporary columns and supports.

> 'We wanted the piers to looks as if they had barely alighted on the landscape, light and delicate – like butterflies' legs.'
>
> Norman Foster, architect

# DECK

The deck is made up of 173 welded steel pieces, topped with a special bitumen road surface. The surface needed to be good for motorway driving – hardwearing and non-slip – while being flexible to allow for changes in the steel deck below. It took two years to find the right mixture!

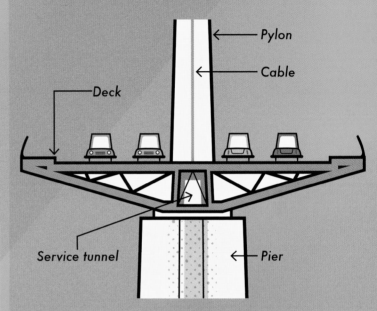

Cross section showing the streamlined shape of the deck support, the four lanes for traffic and the service tunnel.

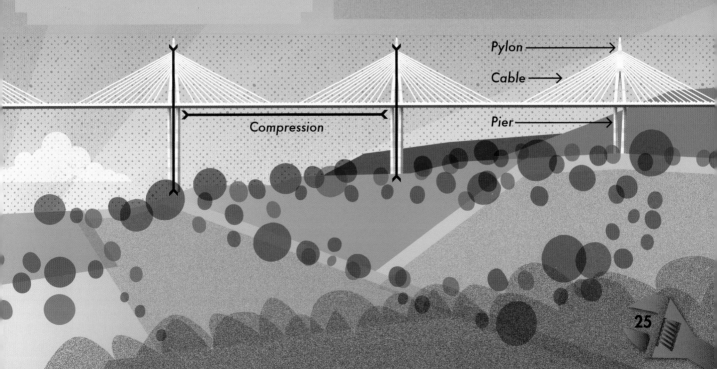

# THE HELIX

The Helix in Singapore is a bridge that crosses Marina Bay. Opened in 2010, it was inspired by the geometric, twisting shape of a DNA molecule. It's a shimmering display of glass and steel that adds a feeling of movement to the structure.

## BUILDING BRIEF

Design and build a landmark pedestrian bridge. It should curve across the harbour and provide shelter for the users from the tropical rain and sun.

**Engineers:** Arup

**Architects:** Cox Architecture with Architects 61

**Location:** Marina Bay, Singapore

## COMPUTER MODELLING

The design for the bridge was tested on 3D computer software. This enabled the engineers to test the difficult helix shapes they wanted to use, specify the shape and fit of each steel piece and accurately plan the amount of materials needed. The software also allowed them to test stress and vibrations from pedestrians and model how the bridge would hold up if damage occurred.

*At night the bridge looks magical, lit by LEDs.*

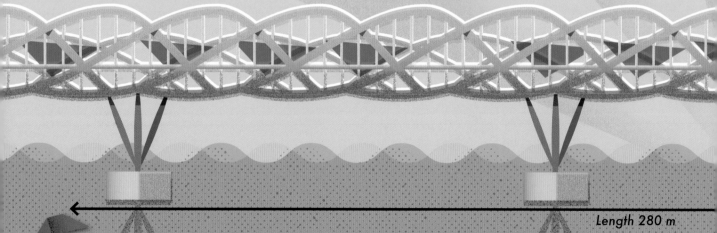

*Length 280 m*

## TUBULAR TRUSS

The bridge is constructed from tubular steel and features two winding helix shapes. The inner helix has a glass ceiling in places, providing shelter for pedestrians when the weather gets too hot or too rainy. The helix shapes are held in place by a criss-cross of steel struts called trusses, which make a super strong latticework frame.

## TRIPOD SUPPORTS

The whole bridge rests on upside-down tripod-shaped tubular supports. Each of the supporting steel columns is filled with concrete and joined to the foundations. The spans in between these supports are up to 65 m long.

'The Helix is truly an engineering marvel. While the structure is incredibly delicate and intricate, it's been engineered to support more than 10,000 people at a time. The Helix is the first example of this structural solution applied to a bridge – there is nothing else like it.'

*Dr See Lin Ming,*
*Arup Project Leader*

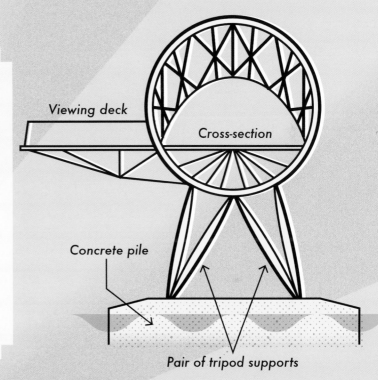

Viewing deck

Cross-section

Concrete pile

Pair of tripod supports

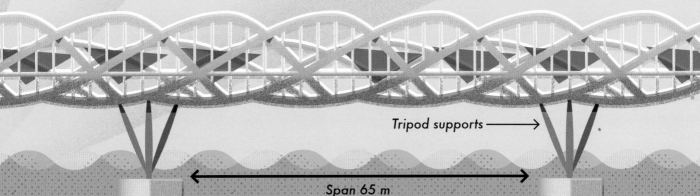

Tripod supports →

Span 65 m

# FASCINATING FACTS

Bridges come in many wonderful shapes and sizes. Here are some fascinating facts about awesome bridges from around the world.

*The* **Gateshead Millennium Bridge** *is a pedestrian and cycle bridge over the River Tyne in the UK. The whole structure tips up with the help of water power, allowing boats to pass underneath. It's like a gigantic winking eyelid.*

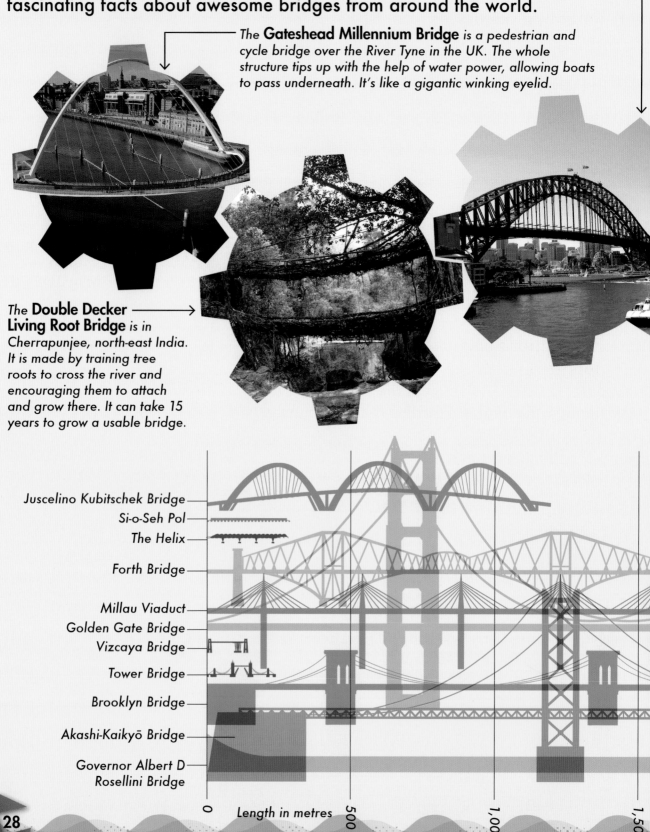

*The* **Double Decker Living Root Bridge** *is in Cherrapunjee, north-east India. It is made by training tree roots to cross the river and encouraging them to attach and grow there. It can take 15 years to grow a usable bridge.*

Juscelino Kubitschek Bridge
Si-o-Seh Pol
The Helix
Forth Bridge
Millau Viaduct
Golden Gate Bridge
Vizcaya Bridge
Tower Bridge
Brooklyn Bridge
Akashi-Kaikyō Bridge
Governor Albert D Rosellini Bridge

0    *Length in metres*    500    1,000    1,500

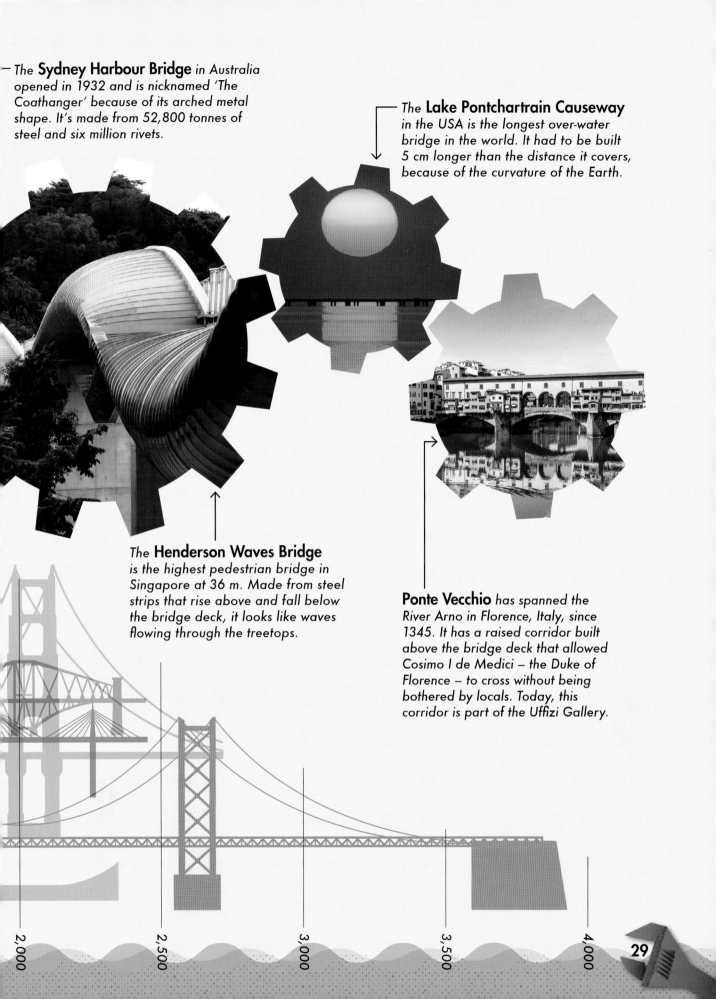

The **Sydney Harbour Bridge** in Australia opened in 1932 and is nicknamed 'The Coathanger' because of its arched metal shape. It's made from 52,800 tonnes of steel and six million rivets.

The **Lake Pontchartrain Causeway** in the USA is the longest over-water bridge in the world. It had to be built 5 cm longer than the distance it covers, because of the curvature of the Earth.

The **Henderson Waves Bridge** is the highest pedestrian bridge in Singapore at 36 m. Made from steel strips that rise above and fall below the bridge deck, it looks like waves flowing through the treetops.

**Ponte Vecchio** has spanned the River Arno in Florence, Italy, since 1345. It has a raised corridor built above the bridge deck that allowed Cosimo I de Medici – the Duke of Florence – to cross without being bothered by locals. Today, this corridor is part of the Uffizi Gallery.

2,000

2,500

3,000

3,500

4,000

# FURTHER INFORMATION

## BOOKS

*Amazing Jobs: Engineering* by Colin Hyson (Wayland, 2016)

*A History of Britain in 12 Feats of Engineering* by Paul Rockett (Franklin Watts, 2015)

*It'll Never Work: Buildings, Bridges and Tunnels* by Jon Richards (Franklin Watts, 2016)

## WEBSITES

The Bridges Database with information about how bridges are built, showing some amazing examples from around the world:
http://www.bridgesdb.com/bridge-list/

How bridges work:
http://science.howstuffworks.com/engineering/civil/bridge.htm

A useful website with information about bridges in Dublin and around the world:
http://www.bridgesofdublin.ie

An article about exciting bridges of the future:
http://www.telegraph.co.uk/luxury/travel/92239/bridges-of-the-future.html

# GLOSSARY

**abutment** A structure built to support the outward pressure from an arch.

**aesthetic** Something beautiful that gives an emotional response.

**anchor** A heavy object attached to a chain or a cable. An anchorage is the place where something is secured.

**anchored** Something that is firmly secured, often using an anchor.

**architect** A person who designs and often supervises the construction of buildings.

**balanced forces** When two forces acting on an object are equal and act in opposite directions to keep an object steady and still.

**bedrock** Solid rock under the soil, clay or sand.

**bitumen** An oily, black tar substance used for surfacing roads and roofs.

**cantilever** A long projecting beam or structure, fixed at one end.

**compression** A force that squashes two ends of an object together.

**concrete** A strong building material made by mixing sand, cement, gravel and water together.

**counterweight** A weight that acts to balance another weight.

**deck** Of a bridge, the roadway or walkway surface.

**designer** A person who thinks up ideas and draws out plans.

**DNA** Short for deoxyribonucleic acid, a long thin molecule inside the cells of living things that carries genetic information.

**earthenware** Pottery made from fired clay.

**engineer** A person who designs, constructs and maintains buildings, machines and other structures, or does the same for engines and machines.

**eroded** A material worn away by wind, water or chemicals.

**force** A push or a pull on an object.

**foundations** The load-bearing parts of a building or structure, often underground.

**gear** A wheel with teeth that slot together with other wheels with teeth. A gear is used to transmit power from one part of a machine to another.

**helix** An extended spiral chain of atoms (an atom is a tiny particle of matter).

**iconic** An object or person that is famous, popular and admired.

**iron** A hard metal extracted from iron ore, used in buildings. Cast iron is a type of hard iron made from an alloy of iron, carbon and silicon.

**landmark** Something recognisable within a landscape or skyline or significant within history.

**lattice** A structure made from strips of wood or other materials that cross over each other in an open but repeating pattern.

**limestone** A white or grey stone, often used as a building material.

**load** The force that a structure is supporting or resisting.

**parapet** An edging wall to a bridge or building.

**pendulum** A weight hung from a fixed point so that it can swing freely.

**pivot** A fixed point in a mechanism, allowing movement of another part.

**plateau** (plural **plateaux**) A flat area of land that is higher than land nearby.

**pontoon** A flat, water-tight boat or structure, used to keep a bridge or other structure afloat.

**rivet** a short metal pin or bolt used to hold two pieces of metal together.

**quadrant** A quarter of a circle.

**shear** Shear forces push in one direction at the top and the opposite direction at the bottom.

**silt** Fine clay or sand that is carried in moving water and often falls to the bottom i.e. the riverbed or harbour.

**steel** A strong, hard metal formed from iron, carbon and other materials.

**stress** Here, stress means the forces acting on a building or structure.

**structural engineer** A person who uses their skills to make sure that the design of a building and the materials used to build it will withstand the stresses and pressures put upon it.

**surveyor** In construction, a person who helps advise on whether a building is going to be safe and strong.

**tension load** A pulling force.

**torsion** Twisting of one end of an object away from the other end.

**tripod** A three-legged stand, used as a support.

**truss** A supporting framework used on bridges and roofs.

**tsunami** A series of huge waves caused by earthquakes or undersea volcanoes.

**welding** A technique of joining two pieces of metal together, using molten metal 'glue'.

# INDEX

# Awesome ENGINEERING

## TITLES IN THIS SERIES: